INDIA
On the Way to School

Anna Obiols & Subi

WINDMILL
BOOKS ™

New York

Ramjed is seven years old, and his eyes are deep brown. He lives in India, the country of the monsoon. This means that for a long part of the year, strong winds and heavy rain cause floods. Every day, he gets up at six in the morning to go to school.

Before leaving, he eats a little food and takes the *thali* that his mother has prepared for him. A *thali* is a selection of different dishes, like rice and vegetables, that is usually served in small containers on a stainless steel tray. In Ramjed's country, people don't use cutlery. Ramjed eats with his right hand, never with the left hand! Eating with the left hand is considered rude.

5

Once he has washed and eaten his breakfast, Ramjed takes his schoolbag over his shoulder and leaves the house with Gigi, his favorite monkey. As soon as they are outside, they see some cows that are roaming freely. In India, cows are sacred, and they are the masters of the streets.

When they have managed to leave the cows behind, they turn right and arrive at the fruit and vegetable market. Ramjed always says hello to the people he knows, with a *namaste*. He does so by bowing his head and placing his hands together in front of his chest. This is the polite way to greet somebody. They wish him a nice day as he walks happily to school. Gigi keeps on jumping ahead!

8

Ramjed's favorite shop is on a corner outside the market: the dye shop. It is there every morning with mountains and mountains of colorful dye on a cart. Ramjed always stops there for a while. Suddenly he realizes that Gigi isn't there anymore. But on the ground, there are several colored footprints that look like his monkey's feet. Ramjed follows them.

"Gigi, Gigi!" he cries as he follows the colored footprints on the ground. He looks for the monkey everywhere, but can't find him. At one point, the footprints disappear and there is nothing left to follow.

Then, one of the elephants that lives in the city approaches. Ramjed passes underneath its trunk, decorated with large, colorful painted motifs.

13

Nearby, there is a mandir, or Hindu temple. Hinduism is the most popular religion in India. Ramjed stops for awhile and approaches the sadhus, the holy men who have renounced everything they own. They are recognizable by their very long hair and beards, and markings painted on their faces and bodies. Behind one of them, Ramjed thinks he sees Gigi. He moves closer, but realizes he is mistaken.

"Where could he be?" he asks himself, worried.

14

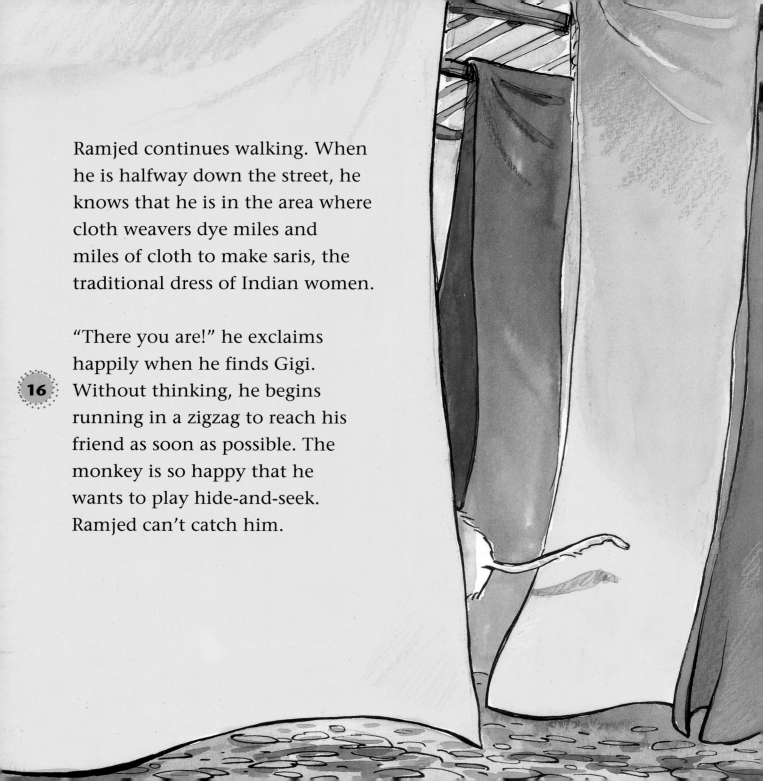

Ramjed continues walking. When he is halfway down the street, he knows that he is in the area where cloth weavers dye miles and miles of cloth to make saris, the traditional dress of Indian women.

"There you are!" he exclaims happily when he finds Gigi. Without thinking, he begins running in a zigzag to reach his friend as soon as possible. The monkey is so happy that he wants to play hide-and-seek. Ramjed can't catch him.

Two streets further away, there is a snake charmer. Ramjed stops to rest for a while to listen and watch the snakes dancing. Suddenly, he has a great surprise. That one isn't a snake.

"It's Gigi!"
This time, the monkey won't escape. Ramjed puts Gigi on his head, and they go towards the school together.

They arrive at a crossroads with several streets. Ramjed can't cross among so many bicycles, rickshaws, cows, people, and cars. Luckily, he has Gigi for these matters. The monkey has a sixth sense and shows him where and when he can cross.

20

When he finally manages to cross, they take the diagonal street and pass in front of a large movie theater. Ramjed loves looking at the hand-painted posters that change every week. Based on the painting, he makes up a story as he walks happily along.

The he passes by some people performing. A musician is playing a veena, a traditional Indian instrument with seven strings. It takes many years of practice to play it well. Some puppets move to the rhythm of the music.

Finally, after passing a man ironing, Ramjed and Gigi arrive at school. He goes inside and greets everyone with a *namaste* and "Good morning." Gigi waits outside until it is time to go home.

At school, Ramjed
learns to read and write
in Hindi and English.
Today, the children
who have finished the
work that the teacher
gave them can play
for a while. Ramjed is
playing with the
Tower of Hanoi.

Many children in India cannot go to school. They have to help their families, work, or take care of younger siblings. Ramjed is a lucky boy, because although he has to walk quite a long way, he is able to go to school.

Published in 2019 by **Windmill Books,**
an Imprint of Rosen Publishing
29 East 21st Street, New York, NY 10010

Book Design: Gemser Publications, S.L.

Illustrations: SUBI-Joan Subirana

Cataloging-in-Publication Data

Names: Obiols, Anna.
Title: India / Anna Obiols and Subi.
Description: New York : Windmill Books, 2019. | Series:
On the way to school.
Identifiers: LCCN ISBN 9781508196365 (pbk.) | ISBN
9781508196358 (library bound) | ISBN 9781508196372
(6 pack)
Subjects: LCSH: India--Juvenile fiction. | India--Social
life and customs--Juvenile fiction.
Classification: LCC PZ7.O1245 In 2018 | DDC [E]--dc23

Published in 2019 by **Windmill Books,**
Manufactured in the United States of America

CPSIA Compliance Information: Batch BS18WM: For Further Information
contact Rosen Publishing, New York, New York at 1-800-237-9932